I Know an Old Woman Who Swallowed a Fly

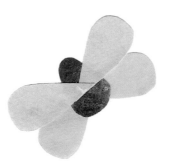

Illustrated by Nikki Smith

If you would like to order a copy of
I Know an Old Woman Who Swallowed a Fly
please contact: nikkismithbooks@hotmail.com
for prices and availability.

ISBN 978-1-4404-8721-7

Published by Nikki Smith Books

For my mom, Nancy, who tickled
when the spider wriggled and jiggled.
I love you

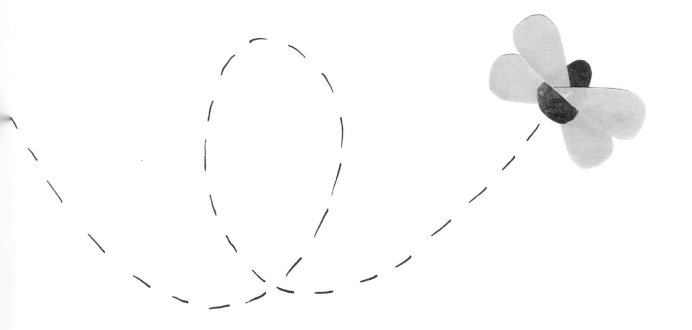

I know an old woman who swallowed a fly.
I don't know why she swallowed the fly,
perhaps she'll die.

I know an old woman who swallowed a spider,
that wriggled and jiggled and tickled inside her.
She swallowed the spider to catch the fly,
but I don't know why she swallowed the fly.
Perhaps she'll die.

I know an old woman who swallowed a bird.
How absurd to swallow a bird!
She swallowed the bird to catch the spider,
that wriggled and jiggled and tickled inside her.
She swallowed the spider to catch the fly,
but I don't know why she swallowed the fly.
Perhaps she'll die.

I know an old woman who swallowed a cat.
Imagine that, to swallow a cat!

She swallowed the cat
to catch the bird.
She swallowed the bird
to catch the spider,
that wriggled and jiggled
and tickled inside her.
She swallowed the spider
to catch the fly,
but I don't know why
she swallowed the fly.
Perhaps she'll die.

I know an old woman who swallowed a dog.
What a hog to swallow a dog!
She swallowed the dog to catch the cat.
She swallowed the cat to catch the bird.
She swallowed the bird to catch the spider,
that wriggled and jiggled and tickled inside her.
She swallowed the spider to catch the fly...

but I don't know why
she swallowed the fly.
Perhaps she'll die.

I know an old woman who swallowed a cow.
I don't know how she swallowed a cow!

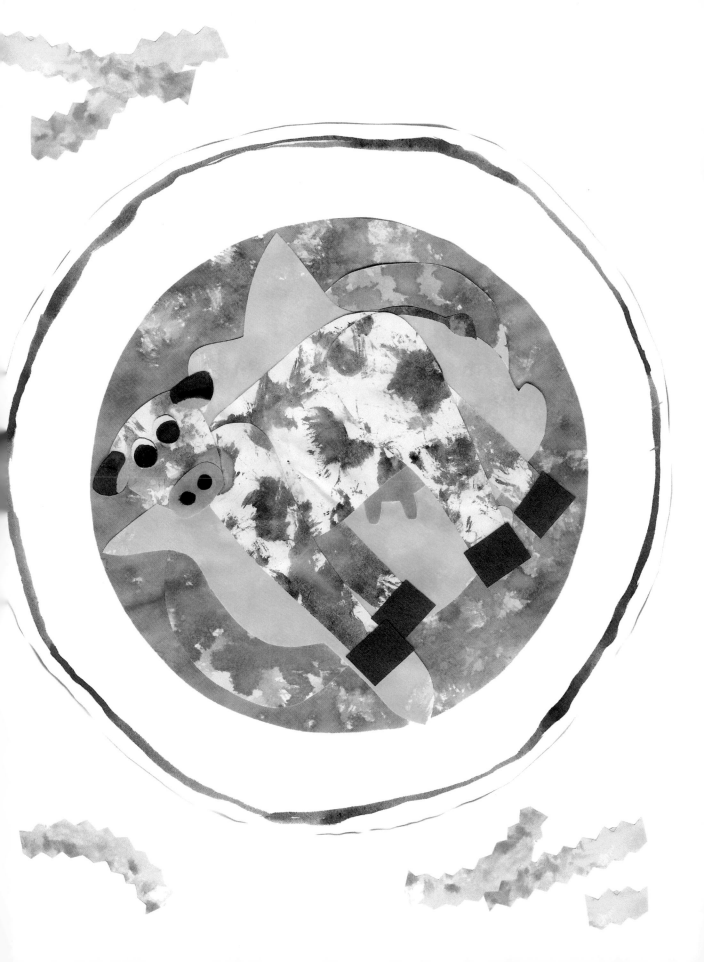

She swallowed the cow
to catch the dog.
She swallowed the dog
to catch the cat.
She swallowed the cat
to catch the bird.
She swallowed the bird
to catch the spider,
that wriggled and jiggled
and tickled inside her.
She swallowed the spider
to catch the fly, but I don't know why
she swallowed the fly. Perhaps she'll die.

I know an old woman who swallowed a horse...

She died of course.

CPSIA information can be obtained
at www.ICGtesting.com
Printed in the USA
LVIC04n2143100214
373173LV00010B/20